P9-CEN-680

DRAG🜨NHEART™

ACTIVITY BOOK

Written by Devra Newberger Speregen
Based on the Motion Picture Screenplay
written by Charles Edward Pogue
Story by Patrick Read Johnson & Charles Edward Pogue

A Creative Media Applications Production

Illustrated by Ihor Diachenko

Troll

A Creative Media Applications Production
Designed by Alan Barnett, Inc.

Copyright © 1996 by MCA Publishing Rights, a Division of MCA, Inc.
Motion Picture Artwork and Artwork Title copyright © 1996
by Universal City Studios, Inc. Published by Troll Communications L.L.C.
No part of this book may be reproduced or utilized in any form or by any
means, electronic or mechanical, including photocopying, recording, or by
any information storage and retrieval system,
without written permission from the publisher.

Printed in the United States of America

10 9 8 7 6 5 4 3 2 1

Sir Bowen's star pupil, Prince Einon, learns all he needs to know about sword fighting from Bowen. One of the last remaining followers of the Old Code, Bowen instructs the young prince to always remember the code. Find out what Bowen tells Einon during his dueling lessons by starting at the sword and going clockwise around the circle, writing every other letter in the spaces provided.

ANSWER:

_____ _____ - _____ - _____   _____ _____ _____ _____

_____ _____ _____ - _____ - _____ _____ _____ _____ _____ ,

_____ _____ _____ - _____ _____ _____ _____

_____ _____ _____ _____ _____ .

Prince Einon's father, King Freyne, is a bloodthirsty king. Notorious for ruling the peasants with an iron glove, he has also made a hobby of slaying dragons. His crested tunic bears the head of the biggest dragon he ever slayed.

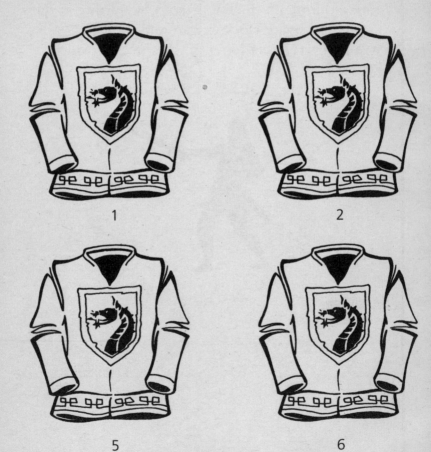

1

2

5

6

Examine the eight tunics below. Can you find King Freyne's crest? It is different from all the others.

3

4

7

8

Decipher this secret code to learn the name of the peasant who slayed evil King Freyne.

A	=	**Z**	N	=	**M**
B	=	**Y**	O	=	**L**
C	=	**X**	P	=	**K**
D	=	**W**	Q	=	**J**
E	=	**V**	R	=	**I**
F	=	**U**	S	=	**H**
G	=	**T**	T	=	**G**
H	=	**S**	U	=	**F**
I	=	**R**	V	=	**E**
J	=	**Q**	W	=	**D**
K	=	**P**	X	=	**C**
L	=	**O**	Y	=	**B**
M	=	**N**	Z	=	**A**

ANSWER: ___ ___ ___ ___ ___ ___ ___ ___

I V W Y V Z I W

Upon seeing his father murdered, Prince Einon goes into a rage against the remaining peasant rebels. But one young peasant is ready and waiting for the prince to attack. To learn the identity of "Buckethead," unscramble the words below and write them in the boxes provided. The letters in the shaded boxes will spell out the identity of Buckethead.

1. I T K E

2. R A I F

3. E R D

4. R H I A

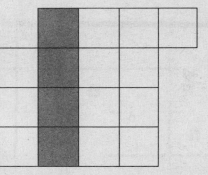

The future looks grim for Prince Einon. His wound is sure to be the end of him. But his mother, Queen Aislinn, is not about to let her son die.

Help the queen and Sir Bowen find their way through the stone ruins to the mouth of the cave, picking up letters as you go. Write the letters, in order, in the spaces provided and find out where Queen Aislinn is going.

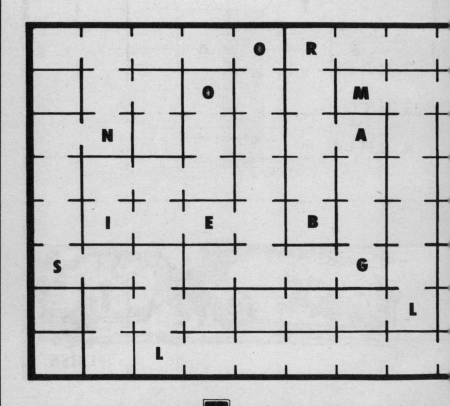

ANSWER:

___ ___ ___ ___ ___ ___ ___ ___ ___ , ___

___ ___ ___ ___ ___

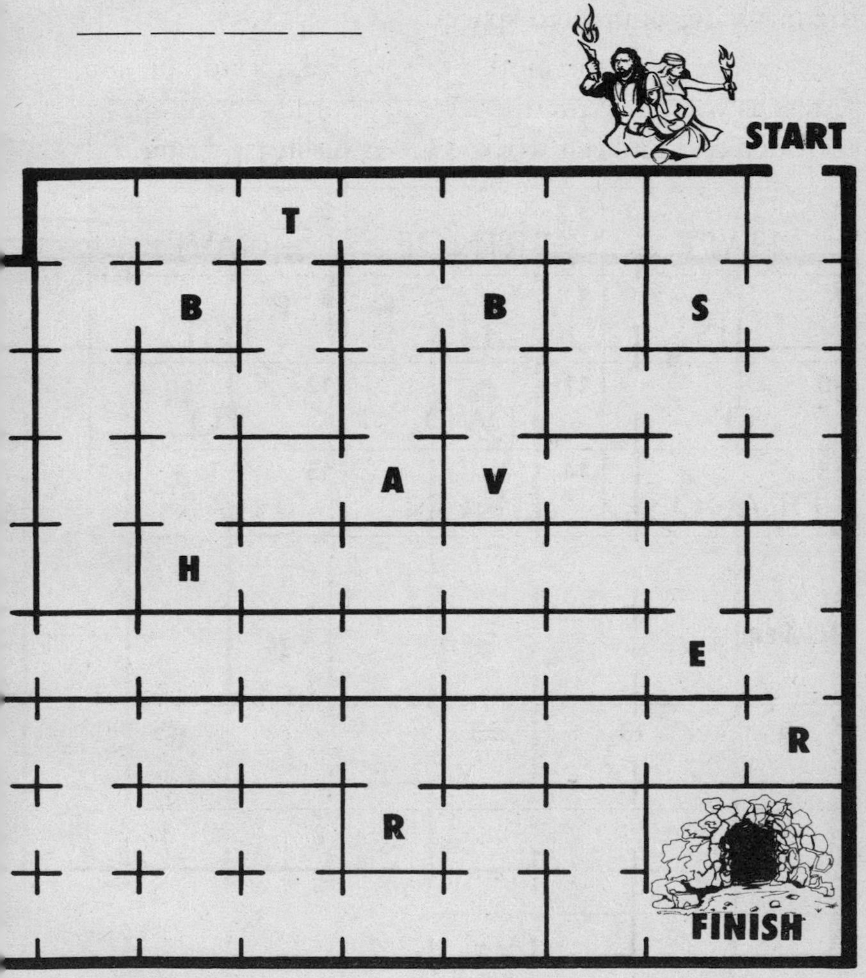

START

T

B   B   S

A   V

H

E

R

R

FINISH

Queen Aislinn begs the dragon to save her son. To find out how the dragon saves Prince Einon's life, take the words in the numbered boxes below and put them in the matching numbered spaces.

1 IN	2 AND	3 SLICED
4 HALF	5 PRINCE	6 GAVE
7 HIS	8 IT	9 THE
10 OF	11 TWO	12 TO
13 DRAGON	14 EINON	15 HEART

ANSWER:

_____ _____ _____ _____ _____
   9   13   3   7   15

_____ _____ _____ _____ _____
   1   11   2   6   4

_____ _____ _____ .
   12   5   14

Sadly, Prince Einon—now the new king—has inherited his father's wicked ways. He has enslaved the peasants, roping them together and forcing them to work in his stone quarry. Luckily, Sir Bowen comes to their rescue.

Each peasant is connected to a letter. Follow the rope to each letter. Go in numerical order. The letter will spell out how Bowen manages to free the peasants.

ANSWER:

___ ___   ___ ___ ___ ___
1   2   3   4   5   6

___ ___ ___ ___   ___ ___ ___ ___.
7   8   9   10   11 12 13 14

How many words of 3 or more letters can you make using the letters in DRAGONSLAYER? We found 82. Can you find more?

_____   _____   _____

_____   _____   _____

_____   _____   _____

_____   _____   _____

_____   _____   _____

_____   _____   _____

_____   _____   _____

_____   _____   _____

_____   _____   _____

_____   _____   _____

_____   _____   _____

_____   _____   _____

_____   _____   _____

_____   _____   _____

_____   _____   _____

_____   _____   _____

Sir Bowen is distressed to see the terrible change in Prince Einon. Convinced that the dragon's heart has poisoned the prince, Bowen has vowed to track down the dragon and kill him.

Can you help Bowen find the dragon in its lair?

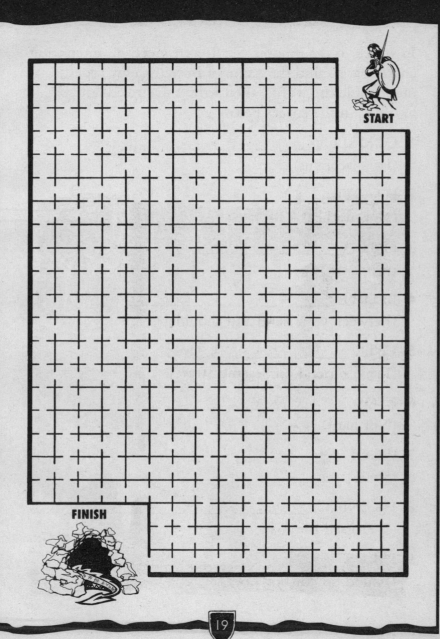

START

FINISH

19

In search of the dragon, Sir Bowen meets an interesting character. To find the name of Bowen's new friend, unscramble the words, then write the circled letters, in order, in the spaces below.

1. OBMRO ◯ ◯ ◯ ___ ___
(For sweeping)

2. HTARFE ___ ___ ◯ ◯ ◯ ◯
(Not mother)

3. FIGT ◯ ◯ ___ ___
(A present)

4. BLOWE ___ ◯ ◯ ___ ___
(Between your hand and shoulder)

5. EBTR ___ ◯ ◯ ◯
(Ernie's friend on Sesame Street)

6. FTOS ___ ◯ ◯ ___
(Not hard)

7. WGOL ◯ ◯ ◯ ___
(Shine)

8. HKENICC ___ ___ ___ ◯ ◯ ◯ ◯
(It crossed the road)

9. PSRUS ◯ ◯ ◯ ◯ ___
(Found on cowboy boots)

ANSWER:

__ __ __ __ __ __ __

__ __ __ __ __ __ __ __

__ __ __ __ __ __ __

King Einon wants a castle greater than any ever built. For six long years he orders the peasants to labor in the stone quarry. There, they spend endless days slaving away to make the king's dream a reality.

These two scenes may look alike—but look again.
Can you find ten differences?

Sir Bowen and Brother Gilbert spot the enormous dragon overhead. Can you match the dragon with its proper shadow?

3

4

Has Sir Bowen met his match? For some reason, this dragon is more difficult to slay than the others. Can you help Bowen chase the dragon back to its lair?

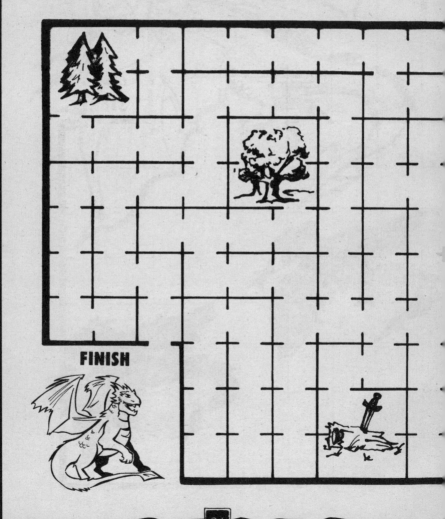

FINISH

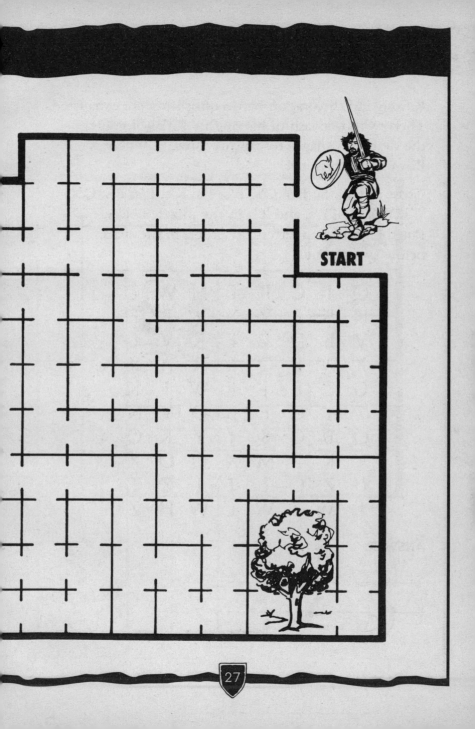

START

27

Bowen and the dragon battle until both are exhausted. Then, with one lash of his mighty forked tongue, the dragon manages to capture Bowen. Where is Bowen held prisoner?

Cross out all the B's, C's, F's, J's, K's, L's, P's, Q's, V's, W's, X's, Y's, and Z's in the puzzle below. Put the remaining letters, in order, in the spaces below to find out.

```
Q  I  C  P  F  N  W  T
H  B  F  V  X  Y  B  E
V  B  D  P  F  K  V  L
X  W  P  Q  L  R  A  K
G  C  P  J  F  W  J  K
Z  Y  C  F  B  O  V  N
Q  B  C  S  J  Y  K  Q
Y  K  P  M  X  Q  O  X
U  Z  C  L  J  J  Z  T
L  V  Z  W  L  W  H  Z
```

ANSWER:

—— —— —— —— ——

—— —— —— —— —— —— , ——

—— —— —— —— —— !

To learn the identities of the unlikely couple who have teamed up to fight King Einon, fill in the two puzzles.

Unscramble the words below and write them in the boxes provided. The letters in the shaded boxes will spell out the identity of the team.

A **1.** Corn on the ☐☐▨

   2. Single. ▨☐☐

   3. ☐☐▨ and arrow.

   4. Opposite of entrance. ▨☐☐☐

   5. Opposite of lose. ☐☐▨

Answer: ____ ____ ____ ____ ____

B **1.** It breathes fire. ▨☐☐☐☐☐

   2. Sound a lion makes. ▨☐☐☐

   3. "An ▨☐☐☐☐ a day."

   4. Tic ☐☐▨ Toe.

   5. Either-▨☐ .

Answer: ____ ____ ____ ____ ____

GREAT BALLS ⊕F FIRE!

Bowen and the dragon have called a truce, deciding
it is better to join forces. Together, they plan to trick
King Einon's soldiers into believing Bowen is a master
dragonslayer. The dragon showers villages with

fire balls, then Bowen pretends to slay him—for a hefty sum of money!

Can you find the two fire balls that are exactly alike?

Kara is hiding in the castle, waiting for the chance to avenge her father's death. Can you find Kara before Einon does?

Can you also find: a dagger, a pitcher, a jester's hat, a man with one shoe, a chess king, a flute, a candle holder, a dog, and a spilled glass?

Unfortunately, Einon captures Kara. To find out where Einon sends Kara, figure out the rebus.

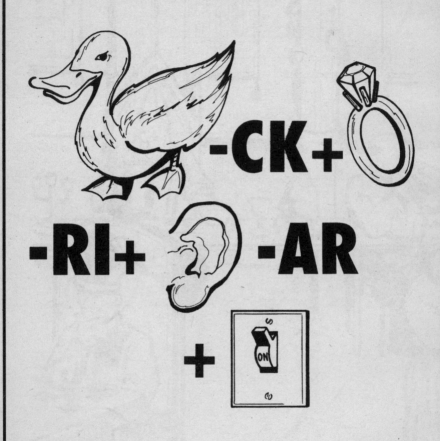

ANSWER:

_____ _____ _____ _____ _____ _____

Now that they are friends, Sir Bowen wishes to call the dragon by its given name. Unfortunately, Bowen cannot speak the dragon's language. So he comes up with a new name. Bowen names the dragon Draco—after the constellation called Draco. Connect the dots to learn why Draco is named after this constellation.

Bowen and Draco are guided by stars. Can you fit all the names of the constellations into the puzzle? We have filled in the first one to get you started.

3 LETTERS
LEO

4 LETTERS
APUS
ARGO

5 LETTERS
ARIES
DRACO

6 LETTERS
AQUILA
CRATER
DORADO
GEMINI
TAURUS

7 LETTERS
SCORPIO
SERPENS
PEGASUS

8 LETTERS
AQUARIUS

9 LETTERS
BIG DIPPER
CAPRICORN
URSA MAJOR
URSA MINOR

12 LETTERS
LITTLE
DIPPER

Kara manages to escape from Einon's prison with the help of a mysterious stranger. To find out who helps Kara escape, find and circle the words in the puzzle. Look up, down, forward, backward, and diagonally. The remaining uncircled letters will spell out the answer.

Find: **KING, QUEEN, BISHOP, KNIGHT, ROOK, PAWN, CHESS**

```
E I N O N W A P N
S O W N M O O T K
N H T E G H R Q O
E U E H S N S E O
E N A I G S I I R
U S B L E I I K N
Q N S H E T N S K
A R C A F R E K E
```

ANSWER:

___ ___ ___ ___ , ___ ___ ___ ___

___ ___ ___ ___ ___ , ___ ___ ___ ___

___ ___ ___ ___ ___ ___ , ___ ___ ___ ___

___ ___ ___ ___ ___ ___ ___ .

After escaping from King Einon's castle, Kara returns to the village to organize a rebellion. But the villagers do not want anything to do with it; they just want to be rid of Kara. Decipher the secret code to find out how they want to get rid of Kara.

A	=	ζ	N	=	μ
B	=	ψ	O	=	λ
C	=	ξ	P	=	κ
D	=	ω	Q	=	φ
E	=	ϖ	R	=	ι
F	=	υ	S	=	η
G	=	τ	T	=	γ
H	=	σ	U	=	φ
I	=	ρ	V	=	ε
J	=	θ	W	=	δ
K	=	π	X	=	χ
L	=	o	Y	=	β
M	=	ν	Z	=	α

ANSWER:

$\overline{\gamma}$ $\overline{\sigma}$ $\overline{\varpi}$ $\overline{\beta}$ $\overline{\delta}$ $\overline{\zeta}$ $\overline{\mu}$ $\overline{\gamma}$

$\overline{\gamma}$ $\overline{\lambda}$ $\overline{\eta}$ $\overline{\zeta}$ $\overline{\xi}$ $\overline{\iota}$ $\overline{\rho}$ $\overline{\upsilon}$ $\overline{\rho}$ $\overline{\xi}$ $\overline{\varpi}$

$\overline{\sigma}$ $\overline{\varpi}$ $\overline{\iota}$ $\overline{\gamma}$ $\overline{\lambda}$ $\overline{\omega}$ $\overline{\iota}$ $\overline{\zeta}$ $\overline{\xi}$ $\overline{\lambda}$!

Draco does not want to hurt Kara, so after making
the villagers think that he has eaten her, he takes her
to safety and they become friends. To find out where
he takes her, unscramble the words, then write the
circled letters, in order, in the spaces.

1. HRSEO __ ◯ __ __ ◯
   (a part of the beach)

2. RETE ◯ __ __ __
   (something to climb)

3. KSAANEPC __ ◯ __ __ __ ◯ ◯ ◯
   (a breakfast treat)

4. ICTKNEH __ __ __ __ ◯ ◯ __
   (a place to cook)

5. TERNRU ◯ __ ◯ __ __ __
   (to go back)

6. OTSHU __ ◯ __ __ ◯
   (opposite of North)

7. DISENI ◯ __ ◯ __ __ __
   (not outside)

8. HIRAC ◯ __ ◯ __ __
(something to sit in)

9. UCUVAM ◯ __ __ __ __ __
(something to clean with)

10. GEALE ◯ __ __ __ __
(the American bird)

ANSWER:

__ __ __ __ __ __ __ __ __ __ __ __

__ __ __ __ __ __ __ __ .

Can you find DRACO in this puzzle fifteen times?
Look forward, backward, up, down, and diagonally.

```
B  F  O  G  Ł  Z  Q  X
O  O  C  A  R  D  P  Y
C  E  A  D  R  A  C  O
A  K  R  D  O  O  M  C
R  J  D  C  R  C  N  A
D  R  A  C  O  A  O  R
O  R  I  C  O  R  C  D
D  C  A  H  C  D  A  O
E  R  A  B  A  J  R  C
D  W  V  R  R  U  D  A
F  G  K  H  D  L  S  R
O  C  A  R  D  I  T  D
```

Sir Bowen, Kara, and the dragon find themselves in an ancient castle. To their surprise, it is the same castle where King Arthur and the Knights of the Round Table established the Old Code. Bowen must solve one simple puzzle. See if you can help him: Draw three straight lines separating the Knights of the Round Table so that each knight is by himself.

The words of the past great knights have inspired Sir Bowen. He is ready to take on King Einon and defend the Old Code. But first he needs an army. Together with Kara and the dragon, Einon prepares the peasants to battle the king's army.

Can you tell which peasant's handmade arrow is exactly the same as the one above?

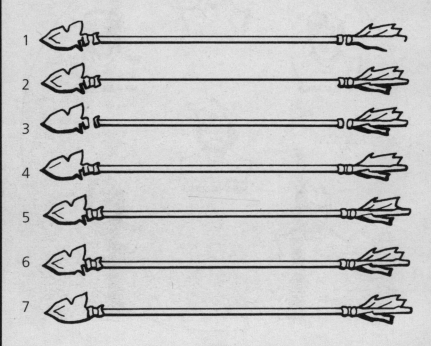

Before leading the peasants into battle, Sir Bowen is presented with a surprise—a breastplate of armor made by the peasants.

Can you match this top half of the breastplate with the other correct bottom half?

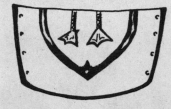

1

2

3

4

5

6

The peasant villagers are finally ready for battle. With Bowen as their leader, they begin their journey toward the castle.

Can you put these words into the puzzle? We have filled in one word to get you started.

3 LETTERS
BOW

4 LETTERS
SUIT
MACE
LOGS

5 LETTERS
ARMOR
SWORD
ARROW
HORSE
BOOTS
LANCE

6 LETTERS
HELMET
SHIELD
SADDLE

7 LETTERS
SURCOAT

8 LETTERS
CATAPULT

CATAPULT

Sir Bowen and Kara share a romantic moment before going into battle. To find out what memento Kara gives Bowen for good luck, put the numbered letters into the numbered spaces.

BRAVERY 13 2	**HONOR** 7 17
GLORY 9	**NOBLE** 15 8
STRENGTH 10 6 11	**PEACE** 5
COURAGE 3 12	**FREEDOM** 4 14
KINDHEARTED 18 1 16	

ANSWER:

___ ___ ___   ___ ___ ___ ___ ___ ___ ___ ,
7   2   9   4   16   6   11   8   3   10

___ ___ ___ ___ ___ ___ ___ ___
1   12   5   18 15 13 17 14

THE A-MAZE-ING DRACO!

Help Draco get to Einon before the king's hired dragonslayers reach him first.

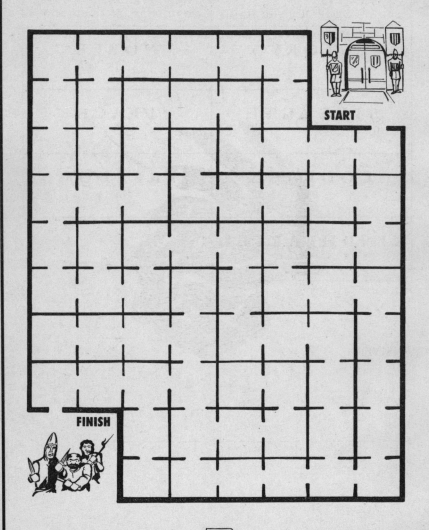

During the battle, Draco makes a tragic discovery.
He tries to tell Sir Bowen, but the knight will not listen.
To find out Draco's urgent message, start at the arrow
and, going clockwise, write every other letter in the
spaces provided.

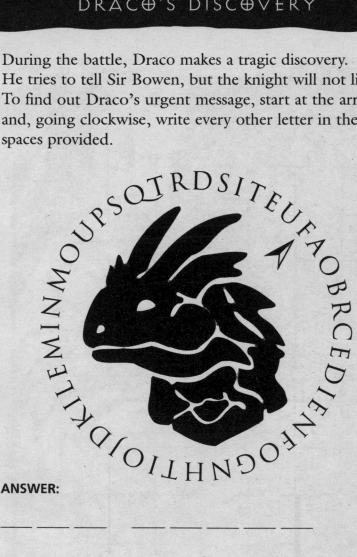

ANSWER:

___ _____ __ ___

_ ____ ___, _

____ ____ ___ ___!

King Einon is prepared to fight to the end. But so is Sir Bowen. To find out who strikes the fatal blow to evil King Einon, take the words in the numbered boxes and put them in the matching numbered spaces.

1 PIERCED	2 FELL	3 MEANT	4 AND
5 KNIFE	6 HANDS	7 CHEST	8 FROM
9 BOWEN	10 THEM	11 KILLING	12 EINON'S
13 BOTH	14 FOR	15 DRACO'S	16 HIS

ANSWER:

_____ _____ — _____ _____ _____ —
12   5   3   14   9

_____ _____ _____ _____ _____ _____
2   8   16   6   4   1

_____ _____ _____ _____ _____ .
15   7   11   10   13

The good guys and bad guys are hidden in this word search. Can you find them all? Look forward, backward, up, down, and diagonally.

Find: BOWEN, EINON, FREYNE, BROK, AISLINN, GILBERT, FELTON, KARA, REDBEARD, DRACO, HEWE

```
I H P N S Y N A N H S T G
L R E V N G E L D M J E D
S K A G G I U O T E O N E
D W E I F E L E C B N E K
E R Z L E R N S C A R A N
X Y A B P Y Y E I D R B O
O H A E E S E A W A R D N
G J H R B M E B N O N I E
V E F T A D W A K P B W A
I N N O T L E F E S D E P
E Y A D Y B H R R N A R Q
```

Page 3:
FIGHT WITH YOUR HEAD, NOT YOUR HEART.

Pages 4–5:
Tunic 7 is correct

Pages 8–9:

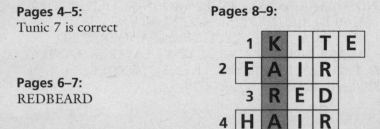

Pages 6–7:
REDBEARD

Pages 10–11:
THE DRAGON'S LAIR

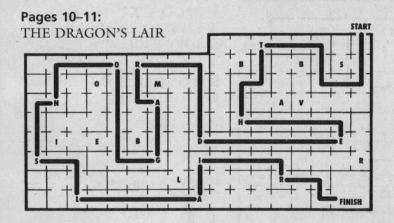

Pages 12–13:
The dragon sliced his heart in two and gave half to Prince Einon.

Pages 14–15:
HE CUTS THEM FREE.

Pages 16–17:

DEAL(S), DONE, DRY, DRONE(S), DRAG(S), RAG(S), RAGE(S), READ(S), REAL, RAY(S), ROLE(S), RAYON, AND, AGE(S), GOLD, GOLDEN, GLORY, GLAD, GRADE(S), GRAND, GRAY, GAS(ES), GONE, GROAN(S), OLD, OLDER, ODE(S), ORDER(S), NEAR(S), NAG(S), NODE(S), SAGE, SLAY, SAY, SAGA, SNAG, SLY, SLYER, SLANDER, SLED, SEAR, SNARE, SOLE, LEAD(S), LAD(S), LAYER(S), LAND(S), LARD, LAG, LAY, LASER, YES, YEAR(S), YONDER, YEARN(S), EAR(S), EARN, EASY

Pages 18–19:

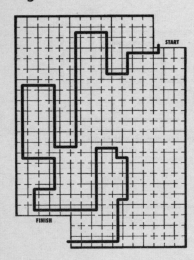

Pages 20–21:

1. BROOM 2. FATHER
3. GIFT 4. ELBOW 5. BERT
6. SOFT 7. GLOW
8. CHICKEN 9. SPURS

**B R O T H E R   G I L B E R T
O F   G L O C K E N S P U R**

Pages 22–23:

Pages 24–25:

Shadow 6 is correct

Pages 26–27:

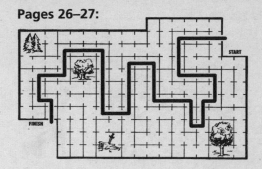

Page 28:

In the dragon's mouth!

Page 29:

1. COB
2. ONE
3. BOW
4. EXIT
5. WIN

A) Bowen

1. DRAGON
2. ROAR
3. APPLE
4. TAC
5. OR

B) Draco

Pages 30–31:

ANSWERS

Pages 32–33:

Page 34:
DUNGEON

Page 35:

Page 36–37:

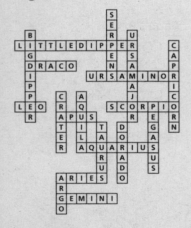

Page 38–39:
EINON'S OWN MOTHER,
QUEEN AISLINN, SETS
KARA FREE.

Page 40–41:
THEY WANT TO SACRIFICE HER TO DRACO!

Page 42–43:
1. SHORE 2. TREE 3. PANCAKES 4. KITCHEN 5. RETURN
6. SOUTH 7. INSIDE 8. CHAIR 9. VACUUM 10. EAGLE

HE TAKES HER TO HIS CAVE.

Page 44:

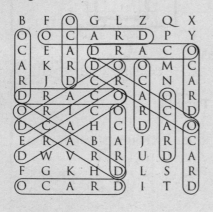

Page 45:

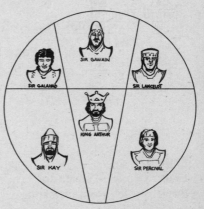

Page 46:
Match 6 is correct

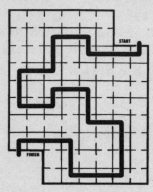

Page 48–49:
Match 5 is correct

Page 52–53:
HER FATHER'S HEADBAND

Pages 50–51:

Page 54:

Page 55:
FOR EINON TO DIE, I MUST DIE!

Page 57:
Einon's knife — meant for
Bowen — fell from his hands
and pierced Draco's chest
killing them both.

Page 58: